T0103996

FIRE

DESCENDANTS OF ISHMIEL

JOSIAH KRANENBURG

Order this book online at www.trafford.com
or email orders@trafford.com

Most Trafford titles are also available at major online book retailers.

Print information available on the last page.

ISBN: 978-1-4907-6951-6 (sc)
ISBN: 978-1-4907-6953-0 (hc)
ISBN: 978-1-4907-6952-3 (e)

Library of Congress Control Number: 2016901461

Trafford rev. 02/26/2016

Trafford PUBLISHING® www.trafford.com

North America & international
toll-free: 1 888 232 4444 (USA & Canada)
fax: 812 355 4082

CONTENTS

Acknowledgements..vii

PART 1

Chapter 1   The Dark-Ones 1

Chapter 2   Magi-Mono 3

Chapter 3   Most Terrifying..5

Chapter 4   His Right Hand...6

Chapter 5   Knuckle-Duster 8

Chapter 6   Tied Up 11

Chapter 7   Please Explain.. 14

Chapter 8   Death Traps.. 19

Chapter 9   Sentron.. 24

Chapter 10   Shocked.. 28

Chapter 11   Powers 33

Chapter 12   Long Drive 38

PART 2

Chapter 1   Descendants of Ishmiel 43

Chapter 2   Grangillion 47

Chapter 3   Captured 51

Chapter 4   Archers 57

Chapter 5   The First Wave 64

Chapter 6   The Second Wave 72

Chapter 7   Angel 78

Chapter 8   Vote 81

ICE (Sequel)

Chapter 1   Mistake 87

ACKNOWLEDGEMENTS

I would like to thank Bryan Davis, the author who inspired me to begin writing this book.

I want to also thank Miss Langford, my teacher during the year I lived in Australia, the year I wrote this book. Also, thank you to all of my teachers who helped with my writing through the years.

Thank you to my brother, Caleb, for always being my biggest fan, and for being the first to read my book on the bus rides home from school.

Thank you to all the people who helped with editing my manuscript. The help was greatly appreciated.

And the biggest thanks to my mom and my dad who supported me all the way. They edited my book, inspired me to keep going, and, of course, are raising me. Without them there would be no hope for me to finish the story and publish it. I love them so much. Thank you.

CHAPTER 1

THE DARK-ONES

J ohn woke up with a start. His mom was kneeling beside his bed, looking at him with a worried look on her face.

John knew what was wrong. "The fire has come?" he asked.

"Yes, hurry," his mom whispered.

John knew about the fire, and the Dark-Ones, but his parents had never told him why the Dark-Ones were after him. The Dark-Ones were always on their way, using a fiery method to catch their victims. But John didn't know when they would actually come.

"Do we have to leave right away?" John wanted to know. "How close is the fire?"

"We must leave now!" Mom was always the worried one. "Your father is already set to leave. Get packed." Then in a lower tone she said, "The Dark-Ones could be here any moment."

They got ready but before they could leave the fire was upon them. Bright blazing flames eating up their neighbour's house. Heat beating at his face, John got ready to leave.

Then a new voice broke in. "You three better not move a muscle! We've got you now!"

John turned around slowly and saw three men in black blocking the doorway. They were armed with knives and had hatred blazing in their eyes.

CHAPTER 2

MAGI-MONO

John froze. He didn't want these men to attack. He was pretty sure that they were some of the Dark-Ones. If they attacked, it would not be a fair fight. Three of them with knives against two tired adults and one fearful kid.

The fire was on their house already. Snapping, popping and blackening the walls. It was altogether way too hot! The men had blocked the front exit and the fire was blocking the back exit. There was no way out.

The fire had come closer, venting out any other thought in John's mind. He needed to get out, and fast! A few seconds more and the fire would engulf him. Bright flames leapt up in front of him, blinding him.

Then his dad spoke. "What are you doing here and why won't you let us leave our house?" He said it to make the men think they had trapped the wrong family.

"You are lucky you aren't dead yet! I really want to attack but we are under orders."

The first man shouted, "Oh you be quiet Larry. You'll give too much away!" He changed his tone and said, "At least Grangillion is doing well."

The man on the left smirked. "Have you even told him why he is the victim?" The smirk grew as he continued. "You let him live without knowing, you Magi-Mono!"

John didn't know what he meant by Magi-Mono, but it was true that they didn't tell him anything about that. "Maybe it is best that I don't know," John said, trying to sound brave. But he definitely didn't feel it.

The fire was surrounding them. John couldn't stand the heat one second more! His skin was peeling and he was choking because of the thick black smoke.

"Do you surrender?" asked the man in the middle. "Will you come to our palace?"

"Never!" John's dad yelled, furrowing his brow. "We are going in."

John felt his arm being dragged into the fire. He knew it was the only way out but he didn't think it was such a good idea to go straight through the fire.

Then John tripped on something on the floor and fell face down in the flames. He had terrible pain in his left arm and he couldn't get up. He felt the tongues of fire eat away at his skin.

CHAPTER 3

MOST TERRIFYING

John's mom and dad, Catherine and Dave, had just jumped through the back door when they realized that John had fallen. He sat there, unmoving. The fire was licking all over his skin. He was in a trance-like state, staring off into nothingness.

His eyes were shining in the light of the fire and his right hand was illuminated and glowing.

"Oh my," Catherine said in a hoarse whisper.

Dave just stood there, gaping in awe.

John looked peaceful sitting there but his eyes and hand were astonishing. The fire had engulfed him but that wasn't why Dave and Catherine were worried.

John didn't know what was happening, but they did. The most terrifying thing someone could possibly go through.

CHAPTER 4

HIS RIGHT HAND

John sat there in the fire. He saw a flash of light. Then another one. Red, green, blue, yellow. There were more flashes, coming closer, closer. Then he saw what they were attracted to. His hand. His right hand was glowing, pulsing red.

He had no idea what was going on. The burning sensation was gone. It felt rather, peaceful. He closed his eyes, not knowing what to do. He suddenly felt different, but a good different. Like his life had just changed, like he himself had changed.

Then he felt a sharp pain. He couldn't pin-point it. It was coming from everywhere, inside his body, even from the air itself.

The fire was still burning but he could no longer feel it. His skin wasn't even affected.

He had to get out!

He couldn't see a thing. The flames were way too bright. He still couldn't get up. But he had to!

Then John had an idea. It might be painful but he had to do it.

He summoned up all his strength and leapt. With all his momentum behind him, he flew right though the fire and through the doorway and he landed on his dad's face.

"Aaaahhrr!" yelled his dad.

"I'm so sorry!" apologized John.

"It's not your fault John."

"What do you mean?" asked John. Then he noticed a black mark on his dad's face. "What happened?"

"It's not your fault," his dad said again. "It's your hand's fault."

John looked at his hand. He touched it. It was hot but just like in the fire, it didn't burn. It felt peaceful. "What's going on?" John asked in an unsteady voice.

"Calm down," his mom ordered, but in a nice soothing tone, "we can explain."

But there was no time to explain because right then the three men in black burst out of the house, looking meaner than ever.

CHAPTER 5

KNUCKLE-DUSTER

"No escaping now! We will attack if you do not come to our palace!" said the first man.

"Are you going to listen to Andrew or are we going to attack?" added the one named Larry, though John could tell that Larry was just trying to get permission from the leader to attack.

"We will never go to your palace!" Dave yelled. "We would rather die!"

"Then die you shall!" the third man yelled back. The three men advanced, knives raised. "There will always be more of us!" He let out a shout and four men appeared behind them.

"Dad, what's happening? What is happening?" asked John.

"So you didn't explain. Typical Magi-Mono!" said Grangillion. "Now he has no idea what to do!"

"That's right but I do know one thing," John said.

"What?" demanded one of the men from the back.

"It has something to do with my hand." John raised his hand for all to see. It was still glowing. There were now more sparks surrounding it.

"Oh my," whispered one of the men from the back. John saw that those men didn't have any knives or other weapons, but they still looked just as deadly.

Grangillion whispered something to Larry about *"the Second Ishmiel"* and *"his power."* But John didn't understand a thing they were saying. Larry shooed Grangillion away.

Catherine and Dave started talking to each other in hushed voices, but John only heard bits and pieces of their conversation.

"What….do?"

"We should….now….his…."

"I think….tell him now."

"…John….surrounded….Dark…."

'They're talking about me!' John thought. 'Probably about my hand.' He kept listening.

"He could….one"

"….possible but….help…"

"Dad. What should we do?" asked John in a worried tone.

"We have decided to tell you everything, even though this may not be the best time, as we are surrounded by Dark-Ones," his Mom told him.

"You will tell him nothing!" one of the men from the back yelled. He ran up toward her and punched her in the stomach. She fell to the ground, wincing in pain.

John saw that he had a knuckle-duster. John looked around and saw that they all had knuckle-dusters. These weren't normal knuckle-dusters. These had spikes!

CHAPTER 6

TIED UP

John froze in horror. His jaw went slack but then he sighed in relief. The man who had punched his mother did not have spikes on his knuckle-duster.

Without warning, two men came up and tied John's hands behind his back, taking extra care not to touch his right hand.

Dave leapt at one of the men and pinned him down. John felt a knife at his throat and the man named Larry yelled, "cut it out. Your son's life is at stake!"

Dave reluctantly let go of the man and stood up. "Put your hands up and don't move a muscle! I'm the one with the knife at his throat!" Then he turned to Grangillion. "See to the woman!" When Grangillion obeyed, Larry yelled to the other men. "You four get the man!"

The four men grabbed Dave and tied him up. Larry pushed John down and bound his legs together and his arms tight at his side.

Andrew came over to Larry. "I'm the leader of this attack so I give the orders. Though you did say exactly what I would have said."

Larry just scowled.

Andrew continued the orders. "Bring the woman to the palace. You know what to do with the other ones."

'Larry wants to kill me right here, right now,' thought John. 'He is definitely the most vicious of the group.'

Even though John was afraid for himself, he was even more worried about his father. The four men with knuckle-dusters were not treating him very nicely. He had already taken a bad hit to the head and the men in black were tying him up very tightly with ropes. The ropes were biting into his skin.

Larry put a gag over John's mouth. He was now tied up almost as tight as his dad. The pain was incomparable. It felt like hornets stinging him all over his body. The ropes were so tight that it felt like he had no skin at all. With the knife digging into his throat, he was losing consciousness quickly. His sight was blurry and a gag was covering his mouth, making it hard to breathe, but he was still determined.

"Stop it!" he yelled, although it sounded more like "Smoffic!"

Even so they understood him. But they definitely did not do what he wanted them to. One man came over and gave him a very hard kick to the head.

John looked around and the scene was horrible. With his vision increasingly blurred, he was slipping out of consciousness quickly.

He struggled to get out, but the ropes, and Larry's grip, made it impossible.

His mom was being carried ruthlessly away and his dad was being bound to a pole. "Set the death traps!" Larry yelled, happy to be giving orders again. Then he turned to John. "The death traps are timers that work one by one. Any death you can think of can be a death trap. If the first one doesn't work, the second one will. If the second one doesn't work, the third one will, and so on. There is no way to escape all of them. It is impossible.

John had some idea of what was happening at that moment, but his mind just couldn't quite process it in this state.

Then John felt a sharp pain in his back, and all was darkness.

CHAPTER 7

PLEASE EXPLAIN

John slowly regained consciousness. He took in his surroundings; he was tied to a pole. His father was beside him. There was pain, excruciating pain. He was in agony from head to toe.

"You awake?" John heard his dad ask. "I think it's time to explain this all to you."

John managed a squeaky reply. "Y-yes. St-start-t from th-the b-beginning."

John's dad continued. "OK, but prepare for a shock. You are a descendant of a man named Ishmiel. He was a great ruler but there was a mysterious box in his castle." He paused for a moment before going on. "When he opened the box, some weird things happened. Some say the box was magical, but Ishmiel believed that the Spirit of the Lord descended on him."

"What?" asked John, his voice steadier than before.

"At that moment power flowed through him. People say it was magic but it was not. Though it was something like that. It was not magic as in witches and sorcerers, but the power of God mixed with the power of the wooden box. There is much to tell you in such a short time but I think this is important." With much effort Dave took a very old looking piece of paper out of his pocket. "It is a promise that Ishmiel gave when he was dying." It read:

I declare that though I die, God will raise another great ruler from my descendants. My power will pass through my line, but use it wisely. No deaths shall come of it.

Here are the signs for you to know who he shall be.

The bottom of the page was torn off.

They both gazed at the page. Millions of questions flashed into John's mind. So many, that he couldn't even process them all. He decided on one question that was the most important and would summarize most of the other ones. "What does it mean?" he asked.

"Some of it I know and some of it I am still working on." He drummed his fingers which were just free of the ropes, as if urging himself to go on. "Many in his line will receive a power to be used for good. The Dark-Ones want to destroy all of his descendants. They have at least one of the signs in their possession, which I know of. They probably have more. The reason they are after you is because on one piece of the promise paper it says, 'he will have two parents of the direct line of Ishmiel.'" He looked at John and continued. "They think it could be you. I think they are possibly right."

"Can you please explain what just happened to me?" John pleaded.

"They are the Dark-Ones. They need your mom for reasons that I do not know. They are possibly keeping her hostage as a trap for us to fall into their hands but then again, maybe not, as they set up the death traps for us."

"Look, there are fire-fighters! Get them to come over!" John shouted.

"No," John's dad exclaimed. "There is a force-field around us. I was awake when they were putting it up. It absorbs sound." He shuddered and continued. "Evil magic."

"So is that why we don't have gags on anymore?"

"Yes. They expected you to scream and cry out, so they put a gag on you. They took it off after they put up the force-field. They knew I would not yell to attract attention so they did not put a gag on me."

John also wanted to know why the paper was ripped but he had a more important question. "But what about the death traps? What are they?"

Dave nodded his head thoughtfully. "Just like they said, they are traps that kill. There are many different types of death traps..."

John cut him off before he could finish. "The man named Larry said anything you could imagine could be one of the death traps. What does that mean?"

"It means what it says. Think of some way to die and they have it as a death trap. They have put many on us but definitely not even a low percentage of all the possible death traps," Dave explained.

John was still confused but he was starting to understand. "I know this is quite random but would they have 'being eaten by a polar bear in the Arctic' as one of the death traps?" John said trying to find something that would not be a death trap.

"Well if that is what they want done then that is what they will do. One death trap could sling you or bring you to the Arctic and they hope you're eaten by a polar bear, or they could bring a polar bear and eat you right there. But that is way off topic," his dad explained.

"So there are death traps set to kill us now?" John chuckled under his breath. "That's encouraging."

"Yes but we will get out." Dave said to John though he did not sound so sure.

John wasn't positive. "But how do you know for sure…"

BZZZZZZZZZZZZZZZZ

"Was that an alarm?" John asked.

Dave piped up startled, "I remember what one of the men said to me, 'When you hear the alarm you know you only have one minute left to live because the death traps will soon befall you.' I also got a glance at the sheet of death traps and the first one is a hidden blade."

He looked around muttering under his breath. "It should be around here somewhere." Then suddenly he pointed upwards. "Up there!" He spoke softly as if trying not to let anything hear him.

John looked up at the tree to the right of them. Up there hidden in the branches there was a fire burning through a rope that was holding the blade. It would soon break, and they were in its direct path.

CHAPTER 8

DEATH TRAPS

John almost freaked out. Was this really the time he would die? The minute wasn't up yet, they still had time to think of something to do, a plan.

"Dad, we can't dodge it unless we get out of these ropes, but I don't think that's possible, especially in less than a minute."

"I think you're forgetting something."

"What?" demanded John.

"Your hand!" his father replied. "Don't you remember that it was hot? Haven't you pieced it together yet?"

John did not really know what was going on, but he had figured out some things. "So, I am a descendent of a dude named Ishmiel, giving me a magical power."

His dad sighed, "Ishmiel doesn't like people calling it magic. Magic is for evil. But other than that, yes."

"So what do I have to do?" John asked.

"Place your right hand on the ropes and they should burn through. But do it quickly or it will be too late!"

John placed his hand on the ropes, but nothing happened. "What's wrong?" John asked, "Weren't the ropes supposed to burn?"

"Well, yes," his dad explained. "You need to believe that you can do it, and you must control it too. If you do not do this there will be dire consequences."

"OK," John breathed. "Just tell me what to do."

"Place your hand on the ropes. Good. Now control it! Force it out! You can do it! If not, it will be our demise."

At first nothing happened, but then his hand lit up with a flurry of sparks. There was a blinding flash and John found himself lying on the ground panting.

"You were just in time!" He heard his dad say.

John was too shocked to get up, but he saw the blade come down crashing into the tree. For a moment he breathed a sigh of relief, though he should have known that it wasn't over yet.

Once the blade hit the tree, spikes came shooting out of nowhere. John was not sure about where they came from, but that wasn't what scared him. He knew now that the Dark-Ones had magic, and surely they would use it here. The spikes had come and they were shooting everywhere. There was no way to get out of their path in time. He saw a spike pierce his dad's leg. Two with ropes attached to their ends stuck into the ground beside John. He realized that they were attached together with the rope. He was pinned down. Two more sets of spikes held his hands down, while two more caught his legs. His plan to burn out of them was ruined. A few spikes without ropes were coming at him now. One stabbed his left arm, which was still stinging from his fall in the fire. At first he had thought it was broken, but now he decided it was not, though it was still pretty painful.

It took a minute for it to end. John looked around to survey the damage to the area. He was fully tied up and he could not move. About two or three spikes had pierced his skin. One good thing was that the bleeding was minimal. His father was about the same, though he had managed not to be fully tied up. He could move his head and one arm, unlike John. Dave had paid for this with at least ten piercings in his arm and legs.

At first John thought it was hopeless, but then he realized that the spikes near his mouth were as thin as knitting needles. He wiggled his head trying to snap the small threads that bound his head down. They were stretching. One of them snapped, two, three, four. Only two more. One on his neck and the other on his forehead. John realized that the further away from his mouth, the thicker the strings were. The string at his forehead was not snapping, but the spikes were coming out of the ground. Since John had snapped the ones closer to his mouth, he would have been able to wiggle the others out of the ground. John heard his father speak. It was faint at first, but then he understood it.

"Don't...pull the spikes...out."

John stopped. Though he couldn't hear well, the message was still clear. Do not pull the spikes out of the ground! John's dad had managed to slip out of his bonds using his free arm. Some of the ropes he was just snapping as John had done, as if they were as thin as wires. He had finally freed himself and was coming to help John. He blew on the ropes and they diminished in size. Then, they were easy to snap.

After a while John was free from the ropes, except for a stubborn one around his neck which would not snap. "They added a little bit of magic," his dad said.

When his dad tried for the fifth time, he fell back exhausted.

John realized that his dad's body would be tired, but since he was almost fully freed he could give it a go.

John wiggled his head and used his feet to push against the ground. The rope still did not snap. John had an idea! His hand was free, so he could just burn through the rope. John put his hand on the rope and concentrated really hard at 'forcing it out', as his dad had put it.

There was an explosion of sparks! He was whipped against the ground, or at least further into the ground than he was before.

When the sparks had cleared John looked up and saw that nothing had changed. Pain shot through John's right arm, pain worse than he had ever felt in his life. Much worse than the pain in his left arm, though it left in a matter of seconds. John looked at his left arm where the spikes used to be, there was no blood and the holes were almost fully healed. John touched the wounds and they healed even quicker. Did his touch affect his healing?

John decided to get back to the task at hand.

He pulled at the rope, but it did not budge. John was wondering why it would be wrong to pull the spikes out of the ground. It was more important to get out than to not pull the spikes out from where they were. If he did not get out now he would be easy prey for the next death traps. John chose to take the risk and pulled. After a few efforts John managed to pull the spikes out of the ground. They came out with a hissing noise, a bit like air coming out of a balloon. John jumped up and beckoned with his hand for his father to come too. John reached the force field and placed his hand on it. Solid.

Dave finally caught up. "How did you get out?" Dave demanded.

John shrugged. "The spikes came right out of the ground."

"Oh dear!" Dave exclaimed.

"What?" John asked. He knew he wasn't supposed to pull the spikes out of the ground, but he didn't think it could be that bad.

"I checked one of the spikes that was in my arm and realized that they were armed to release poison whenever they were pulled out of the ground." John's dad replied. "If you smell the air you can smell the poison."

John took a deep breath through his nose. He smelled something terrible that tingled his nose. At that moment John knew that his dad was right.

CHAPTER 9

SENTRON

"She is awake!" a gruff voice exclaimed.

"Yes. Yes. Though she will be no problem with all the Sentron around!" another voice answered.

"Oh yes, Andrew. You did well with her," he said, pointing to the woman on the ground. "And on your mission."

Andrew continued. "They cannot escape a thousand death traps!"

"Thousands? You didn't set that many. More like twenty."

"I know, I know! But it still seems like a lot. Larry wanted to kill them all. I didn't quite get my way either. I wanted…"

"I am the one you should listen to! I am the one that the master speaks to!" The man yelled.

The woman on the floor stirred.

"She is not fully awake yet," Andrew said.

"No, but she is stirring. She will be awake soon."

"So why did we need to kidnap her? What is so special about her and not about the supposed second Ishmiel?" Andrew asked.

"The master did not tell me very much about this. What he did tell me, he told me to keep a secret," the other man explained.

"But Samuel! Didn't my success today prove me worthy of hearing at least some of the master's plans?" Andrew pleaded, trying to get in on the secret.

Samuel replied, "No! You must still move up in the ranks. You leading this attack definitely showed that you have the talent for leading. You have shown that you were boss there, or so I've heard?"

"Umm...yeah?"

"Well, just because you did well, and even if you move high in the ranks, do not expect to be close to the master," Samuel explained.

"When you said that I showed that I was boss, is that a good thing or a bad thing?" Andrew asked.

"Well, a good boss shows he is the boss, but not too much. He cannot totally rule the mission, at least from my perspective," Samuel told Andrew.

Suddenly a loud alarm sounded. "Sorry, I must go now. Eli and William will come to keep you company," Samuel shouted as he raced out the door.

Eli and William were both on this mission. Andrew had known William for a long time because they were both rookies. As they came in the door, Andrew could tell at first glance which one was William. First of all, he had known him for years, and second, William looked a lot more excited than Eli. This was because he was new and had not proven himself as a very good warrior. He was very happy to go on this very important mission, and now had the privilege to guard the captive. Eli, on the other hand, had been here for at least 13 years and was getting a bit bored to be babysitting a hostage.

They came in chatting. "So, what are you going to do later in your career?" Eli asked in his non-interested voice that he usually used.

"I don't know," William responded. "But I do not think I will be high in the ranks."

"I have heard that you did well on this mission, but that still won't get you promoted," Eli responded.

"Yeah. I'm doing terribly!" William half yelled, half sobbed. "I will never get my place, even if I stay here as long as you have, Eli!"

"Don't worry," Eli reassured him. "If they let you go on this mission, they have to have seen at least something in you."

"Sorry to break into your conversation, but we are supposed to tie 'er up!" Andrew shouted at William and Eli.

They hustled over, quieting up right away. Andrew was not higher ranking than Eli, but Samuel had been sure to tell them who was in charge at the time.

Eli, William and Andrew picked up the woman and began tying her to the pole.

Catherine was lifted up by some men whom she recognized from the attack on her family at her house. She saw the one who had punched her, and the one with the name that she remembered, Andrew, or something.

The men had gathered some ropes and were getting ready to tie her up.

Catherine had been awake the whole time and was listening to their conversation. At first it sounded boring, but later she realized that it could be useful information.

The men probably thought that she was weak, but they were quite mistaken. She could not battle using her power with the Sentron around her, which she could smell. She knew the power against her, the power of Sentron. Sentron is a small, spiky crystal that could fit in someone's palm. It sends off a powder into the air that would prevent the Descendants of Ishmiel from fighting with their powers. Their powers would not work, and if they tried them multiple times some seriously bad things could happen.

She would have to take her chances.

Catherine jumped at one of the men, toppling him over. The other men circled her. She dashed for the door to find that it was unlocked. She sped down the corridor knowing that the men would soon catch up to her. The smell of Sentron was slowly fading, so Catherine knew that she could soon stand a fight.

She continued down the hall with the two men in hot pursuit.

CHAPTER 10

SHOCKED

John did not know what to do. He definitely did not want to die. John wanted to try his right hand on the barrier, but he did not want to get shocked like he did when he tried it on the rope. That was very painful, and it was enough to make him not want to try it again.

"It will not hurt you to try," John heard his dad say from behind him. "Though I do not think it will work."

"So it won't harm me like when I touched the rope?" John asked, still remembering the terrible agony.

"Try it. You can stop immediately if it hurts," his dad said reassuringly.

John reached out and placed his hand on the barrier wall. He felt a tingling sensation. It felt weird, but not painful like last time. John looked at where his hand was and saw parts of the wall melting. The problem was that the poison would kill them before he could make a hole big enough for both of them to fit through.

"It will take too long," John heard his dad say as if reading his mind.

"How else will we get out? It is too strong to run at it." John was getting very worried. After they had escaped the first death traps he had thought that they would survive. Now he thought differently.

"I know how we can get out. Prepare to be shocked," Dave said to John.

"I do not think I can be more shocked than what I have been already," John said determinedly.

"OK," whispered Dave. "Let's just hope that the force field is not a dome. It should be only about twice my height."

John was confused. "I do not know about you, but I cannot jump that high."

"We're not going to jump, silly. We're going to fly!" yelled John's dad excitedly.

John felt his dad grab hold of him and saw the ground disappearing further and further away from them as he slowly lifted up into the sky.

Catherine was getting close to the end of the hallway and she didn't want to be pinned against the wall during a fight.

She turned around to face the two men. They stopped. They pulled out their knives. Catherine was momentarily glad that the Dark-Ones did not use guns.

"Why did you kidnap me?" Catherine asked.

"We do not know but it is our master's orders, so we know the reason is good," said the one named Andrew.

"I'm pretty sure you're here as a hostage to get your son and husband here." Catherine recognized him from before too.

Catherine took a step forward. "Well whatever reason I am here, I do not wish to be," as she talked she took three more steps. It was time to fight.

The woman was now confidently walking toward them. She did not seem to be scared of them at all. Andrew and William raised their knives. Eli came and raised his knife also. The woman was still coming closer, still not afraid. The three men were starting to get nervous.

"Stand back Magi-Mono!" yelled Eli as he threw his knife. The woman easily dodged it without hesitation. Eli grabbed another knife from under his shirt. The men took a step back but stayed in their positions.

William lunged at the woman and she stumbled back. William lunged again, but this time she was ready. She pushed him back at

Andrew. Caught by surprise, William toppled over taking Andrew with him.

The woman advanced again, quicker than before. Eli stood guard as Andrew and William stood back up.

Then with their mouths wide open, the three men watched the woman.

Her body was changing. Her form slowly morphing into that of a beast, a tiger.

It lunged at them.

Olivia was playing at the park with her 8-year-old sister Bethanie.

Their parents, Bryan and Hannah were sitting at a picnic table, deep in conversation.

Olivia was pushing Bethanie on a swing. Olivia was pushing with all her might and Bethanie was going very high.

"You should learn how to swing yourself!" Olivia yelled

"No. I want you to push me!" Bethanie replied.

"How about we go and slide down the slide?" Olivia pleaded because her arms were very tired.

"Yes!" Bethanie exclaimed.

The two girls ran toward the playground. They climbed up the stairs and Bethanie, after Olivia, slid down the slide.

They did this again, having lots of fun. So much fun that they didn't notice a man in black step out of his car and come over to the slide. They slid down right to him. Olivia's parents were so busy with their talk, that they didn't notice him speed off in his black car with their daughters.

CHAPTER 11

POWERS

C atherine sprang at the three men. They were very surprised, and scared. Now she had the upper hand. The men dodged out of the way and Catherine turned back around. They had their knives out in front of them and were forcing her back into the Sentronic area. If she lunged at them now they would definitely stab her and she could not risk that. She had to get her timing right and she could not kill them. She definitely did not want to either. She couldn't bear the thought of injuring a human, no matter how evil. Ishmiel forbade any deaths to come of his powers.

She timed it perfectly. She leapt at the wall and pushed off of it. She spun in the air successfully knocking the knife out of the one man's hand.

He was the one that had thrown his first knife. Catherine chose him because the others would have a second knife and it would be best to disarm one of them.

The knife clattered to the ground.

Catherine put her paw on it and slid it backwards until it smashed into the end of the hall. The man was not worried. The other passed his knife over without saying anything.

'Well at least I'm not being forced into the Sentronic area anymore,' thought Catherine.

She swiped with her claw and quickly drew back.

The man that still had two knives lunged at her, swinging his knives around him. He caught Catherine by surprise, but she shot out her paw which slapped into his chest, pushing him back. His knifed hand swung and struck her in the front leg, close to her paw.

The wound was deep, but when she licked it, it started to close back up.

The men advanced again, pushing her back. Then suddenly she charged forward bowling into them and toppling them over, leaving them sprawling on the ground.

She disarmed them and pinned them down.

John found himself soaring over his small village of Lawrton.

"Dad!" he yelled, "What is going on?"

"I told you that you would be shocked!" His dad yelled back at him.

"No! I mean it! What is going on?" John yelled again.

His dad just laughed in reply.

John felt around his chest. His dad had his hands secured around his chest. He was lifting John. How is that possible? John was good in school and he knew his problem solving, but this, this was just impossible!

Even if his dad could somehow lift into the air, he wouldn't be able to lift John. He was strong, but not that strong.

John was over 100 pounds and his dad wouldn't be able to lift him like this, straight up into the air.

John decided to try it one more time. "Dad, what is happening?"

"Remember you are a Descendant of Ishmiel?" his dad asked.

"Yep!" replied John. "You already explained that."

"And that his powers would pass through his line."

"That too," said John.

His dad continued. "Your right hand is your power."

"I figured that." John was wondering where this was going.

"You also know that I am also a Descendant of Ishmiel, like you and your mom," his dad said.

"Yeah. After you showed me the note, you said that one piece said the special one would have two parents that were Descendants of Ishmiel. You thought it could be me because of that and that means you and Mom must also be Descendants of Ishmiel. Both of you." John explained.

"So we each have a power too, right?" John's dad asked.

"Um…yeah," John responded, not sure what was coming next.

"I can fly," Dave said with no expression in his voice.

Catherine, in her human form, was running down a second hall. After she had locked up the three men, she had fled, before any reinforcement troops could arrive.

She ran down the long hall and saw a sign over the door at the end.

EXIT

'Good, an exit,' she thought. She didn't hear anyone, but just in case, she ran as fast as she could.

Big mistake.

Catherine fell down through a trap door and landed with a thud at the bottom. The door swung shut and locked. She heard an evil laughter echoing all around.

"What!?!" yelled John, "You can fly and you never told me?"

"I had to keep it a secret until you were mature enough," his dad responded.

"Or we are attacked, I get my power, and the Dark-Ones set up death traps all around us so we would die!" John yelled, annoyed.

"We didn't know it would happen so quickly," his dad reassured him.

"OK, OK!" said John. "Let's just land and go save Mom."

"I'm with ya!" his dad suddenly dove to the ground. Near the ground they pulled up and landed safely and easily.

CHAPTER 12

LONG DRIVE

Olivia and Bethanie were buckled and tied up in the back of the man's black car.

Olivia struggled in vain to get out of her tight bonds, but with no success.

They were driving through the countryside. She saw the farm fields whiz by. She glanced at the driver. The man in black was at the wheel driving them way over the speed limit, but driving them where?

"Excuse me sir. Where are you taking us?" Olivia heard her younger sister, Bethanie, ask.

The man at the front was silent for a while, and then he spoke. "That you don't need to know, Magi-Monoes."

Then Olivia joined in. "I'm not sure if you know, but kidnapping is against the law!"

"It is not illegal if the kids I kidnap are Magi-Monoes," the man replied.

"Two things," Olivia said. "One, what do you mean by Magi-Monoes, and two, what's your name?" she asked.

"Well," the man replied, "Magi-Mono is what we call your, um...type. And my name, what's it to ya?"

"I have two reasons for that as well," Olivia explained. "One, we will be in this car with you for a long time, and two, it would be a lot easier to call you by your name."

"In that case," he said, "I'll tell you my name. I'm Grangillion."

"So, Grangillion, can you tell us where we are going?" Olivia asked.

"Yeah," piped up Bethanie, "Please tell us!" She still didn't understand what was happening.

"OK, I guess it is two against one. You win. We are going to the Dark-One's castle."

Olivia heard him mumbling something about being too nice but she was concentrated on something else. This man, Grangillion, is one of the Dark-Ones and was taking them to their castle.

That was where they could not go. They must get out of here. They couldn't fight though her power would give her some advantage, because she was a Descendant of Ishmiel.

John and his dad had gone to the garage to get their van.

"Do you think we will find Mom?" John asked his dad.

His dad replied, "I know exactly where the castle is and that is where they would have taken your mom. I know it."

From then on they were silent. They started to drive toward the castle.

John had one thought on his mind. Save Mom. But with that came the constant fear that they were going straight into a trap. This was what John was thinking as they started the long drive to save his mom.

PART 2

CHAPTER 1

DESCENDANTS OF ISHMIEL

John and his dad had met no interruptions so far. They were stopped at a gas station to fill up because it was a long drive to the Dark-One's castle.

John spotted a black car pulling up not too far away. A man in black stepped out. John recognized him. He was the one with the really long name!

John waited until he went in to pay and then he got out and went to the man's car. He looked in. He saw two girls tied up. One was young and the other was his age.

He tried the door. Locked.

Then one of the girls in the car talked to him. "Grangillion, the man in black, has a spare key in the trunk, it isn't locked."

Grangillion! That was his name. Then John asked, "How do you know?"

"I just do," she responded.

'OK', John thought as he went around to the trunk. 'How did she know where it was?' John thought as he saw it lying there. 'Were they working for the Dark-Ones? Tied up as a trap for me?'

John slid the key into the lock and opened the door easily.

He could easily break their bonds with his power, but he couldn't risk them knowing. 'Aha! Here comes Dad,' he thought. 'Now everything was solved.'

John quickly whispered and explained everything to his dad. He nodded a few times and said, "Grab the ropes and pretend to snap them, but burn them through."

John did exactly that. The girls were so thankful that they didn't even notice the burn marks on the rope or that John was not actually snapping the ropes.

The older girl's name was Olivia and the younger one was Bethanie.

A strong argument erupted. John and his dad wanted to go straight to the castle. Olivia and Bethanie wanted to go back to their parents. They wanted nothing to do with the castle. Though neither of them gave their reasoning about the Dark-One's castle.

Eventually, the argument escalated into a fight. At one point, Dave held Olivia down saying that he was the adult and they needed to go to the Dark-One's castle.

Bethanie was crying and John was close to tears as well. Then he yelled, "We are on the same side! How about you tell us why you can't go to the castle and we'll tell you why we have to go there."

Everyone was silent. Dave got off Olivia. She told them that their enemies, the Dark-Ones, lived at the castle. John told the girls that the Dark-Ones had kidnapped his mom.

"Did Grangillion call you a Magi-Mono?" Dave asked Olivia.

"Yes," said Olivia. "He said it was what they called our...type, though you won't understand that."

"Actually," John said, "You are Descendants of Ishmiel."

"How did you know?!" exclaimed Olivia.

When his dad gave him a wink of permission John explained. "We are too."

"What?" exclaimed Olivia, "Well, OK, what is your power?" she asked.

Dave answered that question. "Fire and flying. What's yours?"

"Mine's kinda hard to explain" Olivia said. "I just know things."

"Well, you'll be helpful when we get to the Dark-One's castle." John grinned, "Because we *are* going."

"OK," Olivia said reluctantly.

Catherine's form morphed into that of a raven, again trying to get out through the trap door. This time she brought a rusty old knife, a few old nails and an old but strong leather strap. All this she found around her in a discard area of sorts.

It was very dark, but a few rays of light came in from the trap door and various cracks around the room. She couldn't get out through the cracks. They didn't lead anywhere.

The room that she was in was fairly big, but not huge. About the size of four spacious bedrooms.

She flew up and stabbed the knife into the ceiling next to the trap door. Next, she hammered the nail through the strap of leather, also close to the trap door.

Catherine flew over and did the same thing about her body's width away, leaving it drooping in the middle. She then landed on the strap and changed back into a human. She grabbed the knife and, strapped tightly to the ceiling, picked away at the door in the ceiling.

Chips of wood fell to the floor below. After a few minutes, she used the knife to pry the trap door open. A hand reached down and, with a knife, cut the leather and sent Catherine tumbling back down to the ground. Before she hit the ground she had an idea.

From the perspective of the men at the top it would look like she had just disappeared, but she actually turned into a house fly.

Catherine flew up and out of the trap door before they could close it.

Little did she know, one man realized that she was a fly and with his bare hands reached out and grabbed her.

Her being here was not going to end that easily.

She needed someone to rescue her.

CHAPTER 2

GRANGILLION

"We're almost at the castle," John heard his dad inform them.

John looked out his window. Nothing but flat plains as far as the eye could see. Except up ahead. There was a large black building. The Dark-One's castle.

It didn't look too big, but his dad had said that most of the castle was underground. There were secret passage-ways that only certain people know how to navigate.

The shape in the distance was now clearer. He could see the walls of the castle and a few positioned guards. This would be hard.

Their van suddenly accelerated. "Why are we speeding up?" asked John.

"Look behind us," his dad responded. John, Olivia and Bethanie all turned as one. Behind them John saw a black car zooming at a high speed.

"That's the same car that we were in when you rescued us," Bethanie said fearfully.

The car was now right behind them. It came side-by-side with them. Then it moved back into the right lane, forcing them off the road.

"I don't give up that easily!" Dave yelled while pushing back onto the road.

The two vehicles kept at this for a while until the other car sped up in front and moved back into the lane.

In a squeal of tires the car in front of them slammed on its brakes. Dave couldn't stop quickly enough to avoid the collision. They smashed straight into the rear of the car, killing the engine. No way to start it now. Grangillion got out of his car and stalked toward the van.

"Out! Out! Out!" Dave yelled to the kids.

They all jumped out and onto the ground. They started to run toward the castle. John looked back. Grangillion was giving chase. Bethanie was falling behind and Grangillion was catching up.

"Dad!" John yelled. "Help Bethanie!"

"Oh no you don't," John heard Grangillion say. He swung around and saw Grangillion latch onto Bethanie's legs, toppling her over leaving her sprawling on the ground.

Olivia lunged at him desperately trying to save her sister. Grangillion was too fast. As she jumped at him he punched straight up at her and she flew and landed behind him. In this split second of distraction, John leapt at Grangillion.

Grangillion spun toward him, his knife pointed at John. John couldn't slow down, he would hit the knife head on. He stretched out his right hand to block the knife. He forced his power out. Maybe if he was lucky, he could reach Grangillion's hand and force him to put the knife down.

Just as he started to push it out, a small ball of flame appeared and shot toward Grangillion's arm. His arm burst into flames and was enveloped. He was thrown back by the force and the heat of the fire, almost crushing Olivia who was getting to her feet.

Dave took to the air and grabbed Bethanie from behind. John helped Olivia up and ran toward the castle, not knowing the peril that awaited them.

Catherine was put into a glass container and the men around her were pointing knives at her. If she transformed, they would be ready.

Someone brought in a shining stone. Its sharp points and clear sides reflected the small light hanging from the ceiling. Someone else lifted the lid of her encasement and she flew out.

'Oh no! The stone the man had was Sentron.'

Catherine was forced to turn back into her human form. As she grew, a few men grabbed her and tied her up. This time, she didn't fight back. There were too many men with knives, she was outnumbered.

She was bound quite tight and could not get out.

"Samuel! Samuel! I need to tell you something!"

Catherine looked up. A younger man had run into the room.

"What do you want?" replied Samuel.

"OK", the young man said. "There are four strangers coming toward the castle. Grangilllion was chasing them in his car. He forced them out and continued to chase them on foot, but just as he caught up they stopped him. It looked like someone threw a flaming object at him and set his clothes on fire and..."

"What! They're getting away?!" interrupted Samuel.

"Yes. But I am just coming to the weirdest part. After they defeated Grangillion, they lifted into the air, at least two of them, and now they are coming this way!" The man responded.

"It's probably a rescue attempt." Samuel muttered under his breath, "Make sure they don't get here!" he yelled. Then to Catherine, "Some people are trying to rescue you," Samuel taunted. "They'll wish they hadn't."

CHAPTER 3

CAPTURED

Hannah and Bryan MacKindly were still waiting in the police station after reporting their daughters missing.

"Your children were in your care when they were taken," said an officer with a name tag that said Mr. Franksons. "Since they were with you, it's your fault that you didn't watch them. We don't even know they were kidnapped. They could have just wandered off."

Mrs. MacKindly responded, "I saw a black car speed off and I could have sworn that I saw Olivia's head in the window." Then she turned to her husband and whispered, "The license plate said DARK 136. All the Dark-One's cars have the same type of license plate. Dark and then a number. The Dark-Ones have our daughters. This is terrible." She started weeping.

Mr. Franksons took no notice of Hannah's tears and continued, "I do not think you are telling us everything. Maybe you got rid of them."

"What!?" Mr. MacKindly exploded! "You're blaming this on us, saying it is our fault because they were in our care, and now you're saying we tried to dispose of them!?! They're our daughters whom we love. Why in the world would you suspect us?!" he yelled.

"Well, we have to explore every possibility," explained Mr. Franksons. "And, it has happened before."

"Well, it definitely didn't happen this time!" Bryan argued, "You can cross that off your list."

"Actually, it doesn't work that way..."

"OK then, how does it work?" Mr. MacKindly asked.

"Like I said, I must suspect everything and everyone. Now, back to where we were before this argument. You are not telling me everything," he repeated.

Hannah leaned over and whispered something in Bryan's ear. "Yep, we're hiding something, but it is something we are going to keep secret."

Bryan got up and opened the door to the police station.

"I am the authority! You must tell me. I am here to solve this crime," Mr. Franksons said.

"Nice meeting you. Goodbye." That was all Mrs. MacKindly had to say before Mr. Franksons jumped backward, unwillingly, out their way.

"Now let's go to the Dark-One's castle to save our daughters," Bryan said to Hannah.

"Yes," she responded. "Even with all the dangers of the Dark-One's castle, we have to go there to help Olivia and Bethanie."

They hopped into their car and sped off.

Dave had settled down and gently set Bethanie down.

"John," he said. "Your progression in your power can really help us."

"Yes, I know," John replied.

Dave continued. "It is getting dark. We should set up for the night. We will take watch in turns. If you are on guard and you hear or see something suspicious, wake us up and I will fly us away to safety. I can probably lift you all. You will be able to see them from far away, because Descendants of Ishmiel have good sight. I will take first watch, and then I will wake John. Agreed?"

"Yes," everyone said.

"Catherine will have to stay for the night. We are too tired to conduct a rescue attempt," Dave explained. "OK. Get some sleep before the rescue tomorrow."

A few minutes later, John was lying to the right of Olivia who was sleeping beside Bethanie.

John felt his eyelids drooping, and soon he drifted off to sleep. And since he was asleep he couldn't see his dad close his eyes, and he couldn't hear his dad snoring. He didn't know that the Dark-Ones had found and captured them.

Andrew stood outside the castle with an army of thirty men. He had chosen ten of them to come with him to meet the intruders head on. The other twenty, including William and Eli, stayed behind to guard the castle. It sounded funny for thirty armed men to come against four individuals, but Samuel had said that they shouldn't take any risks. They couldn't risk the Ishmiel woman being rescued, and there could be more of the enemy hiding out there. Or maybe those four out there were Descendants of Ishmiel and could stand a fight. It didn't matter.

"Chosen men! Advance!" Andrew barked. He then thought to himself 'I'm doing pretty well with this leadership thing. I may not be high in the ranks, but I can definitely lead. Even in big attacks.'

The chosen men were now jogging out to where they had last seen the intruders. Darkness had fallen making it impossible to see more than a few body-lengths in front of them.

"Spread out in a line. Tell me if you find them!" he yelled.

Through the darkness, he could barely see the men disappear into the night on both sides of him.

In a few minutes, he felt the man to the right of him tug his arm and whisper, "We found four of them down there." He pointed. "They're asleep, so we couldn't yell out."

"OK," Andrew responded. "You're in charge of telling the others in the line to come."

Andrew turned to his right and walked until he got to the cluster of guards. There the four intruders lay sleeping. One man, one boy and two girls.

Andrew leaned down and injected each of them with a type of tranquilizer. "That should last," he determined.

"Get out the scanner," he said to one of the others.

A man pulled out something from his shorts. It was black with a big black button on the top. It also had a blinking red light, (similar to the device that scans your groceries at the store).

The man pressed the button and a horizontal line of red shot out. He passed it over the man first. The red light on the scanner started flashing rapidly.

"Magi-Mono," said the man with the scanner.

"As I suspected," Andrew said. "Next one."

He shone the scanner light on the boy now. The indicator light again sped up the flashing. "Another Magi-Mono."

"Wow. Two in one. Caught sleeping. We are very lucky to get two!" Andrew exclaimed.

The next to be scanned was the older girl. The scanner gave the same response with the girl as with the other two. "Magi-Mono," the man said again.

This surprised Andrew. "Three. Why would the man have brought them here? Why? I guess the other one is one too! Check her!" he pleaded.

Again they scanned, and again the scanner gave the rapid flashes of a Magi-Mono. "Yep. You were right. Another Magi-Mono."

"Wow! Four Magi-Monoes!" Andrew cried out.

By now the other men in the line had arrived.

"All of them are Magi-Monoes!" Andrew explained to the newcomers. "Bring them to the castle. We'll have five! What a day!"

The men hurried to do what he said. Three men each grabbed a child, but it took two to carry the man away. Because of the tranquilizing solution in them, none of the Magi-Monoes awoke on the way to the castle, or even while being securely tied up.

CHAPTER 4

ARCHERS

When John came-to, he couldn't remember where he was. He wasn't at home in his bed. He was standing vertically and his upper arms were stuck tight to his side so that he could only move them from the elbows down.

Then he remembered his dad taking first watch and himself going to sleep... on the terrain of the Dark-Ones' castle...The Dark-Ones' castle!

Suddenly John was fully awake. He looked around. He was right, they were *inside* the Dark-Ones' castle. Olivia was tied up on his left, and his dad was on his right, with Bethanie further along beside him.

And beyond her was John's mom, Catherine.

John wanted to yell out, but he knew he couldn't. Instead he started to burn through the ropes, which was easy, because of the progress of his power. He had fully freed his arms when he caught a strong scent in the air. Something in his brain was yelling, 'Stop it! Stop it!' He stopped burning the ropes and he instantly felt better. John didn't know, but it was Sentron he was smelling. It was a very good thing that he stopped, for two reasons. One was because the smell was of Sentron, and the other is that a man in black burst into the room right that second. John pretended to still be tied up.

The guard had already seen that he was awake, so it wouldn't do any good to pretend to be asleep. Instead, John decided to look out the only small window in the enclosed brick room.

Outside, John could see the sun coming up. It was morning. He kept looking and saw where they had slept and their van, smashed, at the side of the road.

"Thought ya could win, did ya?" said the guard from behind him. "Well ya can't!" he exclaimed as he waved a spiky rock under John's nose. The smell suddenly strengthened. It smelled a bit like a mixture of freshly cut grass and metal. "Just a bit of Sentron keeps you from having a chance," the guard continued.

John thought back to his most recent birthday. His parents had sat down with him and told him about the Dark-Ones. He hadn't understood much, but he remembered them saying something about Sentron. John thought harder but he couldn't remember anything else.

"...And Ishmiel was very smart at not letting you kill anyone," the man smirked. "He sure saved a lot of us with that curse."

John remembered the note his dad had showed him. He specifically thought back to the part the guard was referring to. *No deaths shall come of it.* But it was referring to our powers, not us in general. 'What would happen if deaths came of our powers?' John thought.

John decided just to ignore the guard. He looked out the window again. What he saw astounded him. A red sports car was speeding toward the castle. Behind it were five police cars, sirens blaring. John could just hear the sirens now.

John turned away pretending not to have seen anything, but there was probably a look of surprise on his face, and the guard then looked out the window.

John heard yelling from below him.

The guard scrambled out the door, not bothering to close it behind him. The Sentron left with him.

Hannah stuck her head out of the sunroof of their car. When she looked back she saw the five police cars pursuing them. Since she was a Descendant of Ishmiel, she could control other people, but only one at a time. She concentrated on the driver of the lead police car. He slammed on his brakes. The cars behind rammed into that car, forcing the police inside to get out and run after them.

The castle wasn't far ahead.

She turned to face the castle guards. One-by-one they would drop to the ground with a bone-breaking force, or cut themselves with their own knives, or turn to their neighbour to fight, or turn and run, smacking right into the castle walls.

She reached down and gave her husband a high-five. Then, looking back, she saw roughly twenty archers on the roof of the castle. As one, they fired their arrows.

Hannah quickly ducked back into the car and closed the sunroof. The archers had deadly aim, even at a moving vehicle. One arrow shattered the windshield. Four others pounded the roof and sunk in.

Hannah got back out. Maybe she could stop the archers before they took a second shot!

She opened the sunroof and stood up. She smelled something metallic. Sentron.

She managed to pull out one of the arrows. On the end, there was Sentron. If one of those arrows hit her, she would never be able to use her powers again. Well, there is a cure, but a near impossible one. Anyway, with the Sentron present, she couldn't use her power. That was probably why they shot the arrows, not to hurt her but to disable her.

"There is Sentron on the arrows," she said to Bryan, "Let me get out."

"But then you will be an easy target for the archers' arrows," he responded.

"Just let me out, there is Sentron here so I am of no use if I stay behind. Out there I can fight.

"Fine," Bryan said as Hannah got out the door of the car. "I can defend myself," he said as he patted a case under the passenger seat. She quickly ran away from the car and from the Sentron.

Soon she was far enough away from the Sentron to use her power. She downed a few archers, but the rest fired. It was a rain of arrows. Hannah wouldn't be able to get away in time. She quickly hid behind a small tree, hoping it would save her from the arrows, but it was too small to cover all of her. She stood still in the shower of arrows.

John had seen the fallen guards, and he watched the people in the red car come. He saw the police running because their cars had crashed. He saw the arrows pounding into the roof of the red car. He stopped watching when the woman left the car.

After that, he turned to more important tasks, freeing the others.

By now he had awoken them all and had freed his mom and Bethanie, and he was now working on his dad.

Bethanie had run to the window to watch, then she yelled out. "There's Mommy over there by the tree, and Daddy is the one driving the car! They've come to save us!"

John hurried up on his dad. Because of his rush John accidentally set his dad's clothes on fire.

"Ouch!" Dave yelled.

"Sorry" John said, batting out the flames.

Soon he had freed him and he went over to Olivia.

She already had her arms freed, and the ropes at the top of her chest and at her neck were snapped. She bent over and reached around the ground until her fingers caught hold of an old, rusty dagger. She began cutting at the remaining ropes. When she was done, Olivia looked up and saw that John was watching her. A look of embarrassment was on her face.

"Some things I just know," she said, "Like, how to free myself."

It was true. She had gotten out all by herself.

"Now that we are all free…" Dave was cut short by the look of horror on Bethanie's face.

"They shot at Mommy with their arrows."

The two adults and three children ran out the open door and down the staircase. Olivia's eyes were darting everywhere, Catherine was now in the form of a tiger. This didn't surprise John because of all the other things that had happened to him. Dave was hovering just above the ground and John himself had his right hand hot and at the ready.

This would be the biggest fight yet.

Samuel stepped out onto the roof in time to see some of the archers fall. "Men. Fire!" he yelled. Both the Sentronic arrows and the normal arrows flew out at the Magi-Mono who was on the terrain. A few more archers ran or smacked their heads against the ground, without explanation.

The Magi-Mono hid behind a tree, but the tree was much too small to save her. Most of the arrows pounded into the tree, but one caught her in the arm.

"Archers!" he yelled, "Grab your knives and swords and finish the fight with those evil ones!"

All of them left, except two.

Samuel looked down in time to see the prisoners escaping. "The Magi-Monoes have escaped! You two, gather all forces for this fight!"

Hannah stood back up with the arrow in her arm. There was a second of panic before she realized that it was not Sentronic. She got out a knife and, wincing in pain, cut out the arrow. She cut some of her clothes and tied it around the wound, knowing it would heal quickly. She was well enough to fight. She had to fight. She had to save her daughters.

CHAPTER 5

THE FIRST WAVE

Hannah ran toward the others to join forces. Though she had little time to reunite with her daughters, she hugged and kissed them, reassuring them that all was under control.

Out of the castle's front door came about fifty men in black with knives and about ten with swords.

Hannah quickly got to work on them, but during this she forgot about the one archer that was left.

On his second shot he hit her in the leg. On his fifth shot he hit her on her shoulder and she fell over, unable to continue fighting.

One down.

Samuel watched as the woman fell. She was first priority because of her controlling power.

The police had already been taken care of thanks to their catapult, using up their only large ammunition.

The father of the two girls had a gun. That's annoying. He had to be next.

Samuel continued watching as the first wave, with now about fifty men, continued forward.

The flying man was dropping stones on the army, knocking them out one by one. When they pass him, they would come to the boy, the Second Ishmiel who would set their clothes on fire. But he was slow, not a problem.

If a man could get to the girls the older of the two would fight with her knife. She was quite good with it, but not as good as the men.

If this happened, the flying man would drop a rock on him and that fight would be over.

The man with the gun did not get many good shots, but when he did, one of the black men fell.

About seven men had surrounded the shape-changing woman. Now she was a tiger. That would be a good fight, but the men would probably win.

The remaining twenty men dodged the falling rocks and shoved past the boy and the older girl.

They pinned the little girl down, threatening to kill her, and told everyone to stop fighting. They did.

Samuel couldn't hear exactly what they were saying from up there on the castle, but when they gestured for the man to drop his gun and come, he didn't argue.

As he was coming, one of the men stuck the girl with a tranquilizing needle.

Two down.

Bryan dropped his gun and jogged to his daughter, who was surrounded by the men.

One of the men stuck a needle into Bethanie. "Hurry up!" he yelled, "or I'll kill her!"

Bryan bolted and stood beside his daughter in no time.

"Lay down beside her, NOW!" the man yelled.

He did so.

The man stuck a needle into his arm and he quickly lost consciousness.

Three down.

Only four fighters left.

Catherine had watched Hannah go down by an arrow and Bethanie being overtaken. Then she saw Hannah's husband being forced by fatherly instinct to go over to his daughter, and then him being put to sleep.

She was now surrounded by seven Dark-One's.

Now it was her turn to fight!

She had easily fought off three men but now there were seven. This would be a challenge.

She leapt forward, knocking two men to the ground and turned back to the others. She pressed her front claws into the men on the ground so they couldn't get up. One man ran at her, jumped and stabbed her in the shoulder.

Catherine grabbed him in her jaws and flung him away. The gash in her shoulder sent jolts of pain through her entire body.

She also flung away the two men who were under her paws in order to focus on the others

Now there were only four left. Easy.

Catherine flung two more away, but it resulted in two more stabs.

The first stab-wound had almost healed because of her Ishmielic blood. The two new wounds were deep and blood oozed out. Soon they would also heal up....hopefully.

She turned to face the last two men. At first they looked scared but soon a look of confidence and evidence of smirks took over their faces.

"Look out Mom!" Catherine heard John yell from behind her.

Catherine turned soon enough to see a man take a needle out of her hind quarters.

Her vision began blurring and soon she collapsed in a heap.

Four down.

Olivia struggled as five men held her down. John and Dave were doing their best to keep the others away.

She saw that Catherine was now asleep, but that was the least of Olivia's problems.

With her knife, Olivia cut a man's leg and then another.

The other men dispatched her by knocking her out cold with the blunt end of the knife.

Five down.

"Dad!" John yelled, "Do you think you can carry me? I can probably ignite their clothes from up there."

"If I come down to get you, I won't be able to defend myself, and if I'm holding you, I can't drop rocks," he explained.

"OK," John replied.

"It's only us now," Dave yelled to John with a hint of uncertainty in his voice.

"I know," John said." I don't think we can win this."

"Don't give up hope!" Dave yelled encouragingly.

Dave continued dropping stones, and John continued to set fire to the men's clothing. Some men couldn't stand the heat of the fire, but most put it out and continued to fight. Many of the men that were hit by a rock were instantly knocked out cold. A few of the men dodged the rocks and came closer.

"Come on, John," Dave yelled down. "Keep it up."

John stopped for a moment and pushed his right arm outward. A fireball appeared in his hand. He quickly threw it at the closest man. He burst into flames.

"Well done John," his dad said. "Keep it up."

Dave watched as John continued throwing fire balls at the remaining twelve men. John was doing really well, but he also provided a distraction. All the men were watching John, not Dave. He could drop stones undetected because they were concentrating on John.

This was all working perfectly until one man pointed up and ordered, "Kill him first! If we get rid of him, we can fight the Second Ishmiel alone!"

At that point, five men threw their knives. Dave dodged three and blocked two others with a fairly large rock. Then they threw again, but this time Dave wasn't fast enough to dodge all of them. Two of them got through, one hit his leg and the other hit his upper arm. Dave lost his control and fell to the ground with the rock on top of him, pinning him down.

Six down. One left. The Second Ishmiel.

John ran to his dad. Good. He was alive. He turned back to the remaining men burning with pure hatred.

John created another fireball in his right hand and flung it with all his might in the direction of the Dark-Ones.

It bowled into the first three men and sent them sprawling. Their clothes were aflame and they rolled painfully on the ground in an attempt to extinguish the flames. The fireball continued and slammed into five more with its intense heat that made them crumble into a heap.

The two men that were left ran, but John quickly and easily threw smaller fire balls and knocked them over.

John ran around checking his friends and family. His mom, Bethanie, and her dad were asleep and would likely remain that way for a few hours. His dad and Olivia's mom were doing OK, and Olivia had a bad bruise but she was starting to come to.

Even all the Dark-Ones were still alive, including the ones John had burnt, though most were now physically scarred for life.

John gathered all of his friends and parents together so he could protect them all.

Just at that moment he heard something behind him. He turned around and saw about forty more Dark-Ones charging toward him.

CHAPTER 6

THE SECOND WAVE

'O h no!' thought John, 'a second wave!' He had feared this, but now it had happened!

"I'll be back," John said to his unconscious friends.

John ran forward, launched a large fireball, taking out a few men, and grabbed a knife from one of the fallen soldiers.

He ran on and launched a few more weak fire balls. Twenty men ran at him as eight stayed back.

Fifteen men surrounded him and the other five advanced. John threw two fire balls at the advancing men. They caught fire and fell over. The fifteen other men slowly came closer and closer to John. If John shot at one side the other side would catch him or even kill him.

John spotted two familiar faces in the group. He had a good memory and recognized them as Andrew and Larry. One on each side of the circle. John remembered how terrible Larry was. His next move would be risky.

He sent a small, but strong fire ball that way and quickly turned to the others. They had advanced, but stopped when he spun back around. If they all rushed in at once they could easily take John down, but they seemed scared. 'They're scared of me!' John realized.

Then John had a great thought. If I can create fire balls and throw them I can probably do other things with fire too! John summoned up all of his energy and shot fire in a ring into the ground that surrounded him. From that ring sprang flames reaching higher than the tallest man!

The Dark-Ones stumbled back with fright.

John could see right through the fire and the heat didn't bother him one bit. John could even shoot through the flames, his balls of fire even growing while passing through the wall of flames.

John was getting tired and the fire balls weren't as big as they had been earlier in the battle, but he could 'keep it up', as his dad had put it.

The Dark-Ones had now recovered from their shock and decided on a different plan. They started to throw their knives right through the fire, in a direct path toward John.

Samuel watched from above. Oh no! The Second Ishmiel is still standing. His power has increased.

Samuel saw another wave of Dark-Ones charging out now. Good. They would easily overtake him.

He watched as they surrounded the kid. This was a good attack because if the Second Ishmiel shot one way, the other side could advance on him. If he chose not to shoot, the men would be on him in no time.

Then the kid did something very unexpected. He created a curtain of flames around himself. Apparently the flames were very hot because the men all jumped back. After their moment of shock, Samuel saw his men throwing their knives through the fire.

What!? Didn't they know that they couldn't kill a Descendant of Ishmiel? That's why we have been capturing them. Fools!

Samuel watched as the knives flew. Then he noticed something unusual about the flames.

John saw the men throw their knives. He couldn't run out of the circle of flames because if he did he would be in plain sight of the Dark-Ones. John did the only thing he could do. He pushed out his power with all of his might.

The fire around him spun in a fiery inferno.

Then the knives flew in, but the flames were so hot and so powerful that the knives, metal though they were, couldn't get through. With some, the hilts burnt and melted. With the others the power of the flames batted them way off course. The circling of the flames was much too powerful for the force of the knives. By this time John was too tired to 'keep it up'.

He lowered the flames, so that he could see over them. When he looked, he saw that the men had backed further away because of the heat of the fire. They started advancing again.

John shot out some weak fire balls that knocked a few men down. The other men threw their knives and John made a run for it.

A few men didn't have any knives left so they ran toward the castle to get more.

Six men continued advancing. The eight men who had left earlier stood ready, not far off.

The six men started running after John. John was fast, but the men were faster, and were slowly catching up. It was a good thing John was one of the fastest in his class back home, because if he was slow, the men would have caught him by now.

John stuck the knife he had gathered into his pocket, then he grabbed a sword from a fallen man, put it in his left hand and turned toward the remaining men.

He threw four small fireballs which slammed into those men.

Three men got up and stalked toward John. He brought up all the energy he could muster and quickly threw another fireball. Two men were down with that one, but one still stood strong.

John tried to create a fire ball, but only a tiny flame leapt up. The flame was quite hot, but too small to bring down a man. John snuffed it out and lifted the sword into the air with a struggle. He couldn't believe the weight of it.

He let gravity take over as the sword came crashing down on the weapon arm of the Dark-One. The man started to crawl away, but John hit him on the head with the flat side of the sword. The man fell flat on his face. The remaining men had supposedly figured out that John couldn't create fire at that moment so they advanced at him again.

John had to decide what to do. He could run or he could fight, but he had to make the decision quickly because the men were almost upon him.

'How did he escape them? Is his fire so powerful?'

Samuel watched as fireball after fireball plowed into the men. When only the eight spare men and one advancing man were still up, the Second Ishmiel stopped hurling his flames.

Why did he stop? Was his power drained? If so, that was good. The remaining men could easily take him down now.

He saw the boy hold up a sword and knock the knife out of the man's hand. He then knocked him unconscious with the flat side of the blade.

The eight other men started advancing because they knew he couldn't create fire now. The Second Ishmiel stood his ground, facing the men. Then Samuel saw something horrific.

Dave woke up with a stinging pain shooting through his body. He checked his stab wounds. They weren't open, but the pain was terrible. He also checked his chest where the rock had fallen. There could have been a broken rib, but he was healing already.

Dave realized that he must have been unconscious. He checked his head for bumps. Only a small one, not much, there was probably no permanent damage.

Dave then looked to his side and saw John battling some men. He tried to get up but he couldn't. All he could do was pray for him. 'Dear God,' he started, 'please help my son. For the last few days he has faced enormous trials. He is now fighting evil men who go against Your Holy ways. Please send Your Guardian Angel to help him and lead him on his way. Thank you Lord for bringing us through all these trials and please help us through the next ones. Thank you for giving John the strength and the courage of a true Descendant of Ishmiel and a follower of You. In Your Holy Name, Amen.'

CHAPTER 7

ANGEL

Samuel stared in awe at the thing that had appeared. It looked like a man, but it was tall and bright.

Samuel had to squint to look at it. What is it? Who is it? It had a flaming sword in its hand which he brought down on the men and they laid there motionless.

The boy didn't look affected until there was a blinding flash and both he and the boy had to look away. When Samuel looked back down, there was a normal man in the place of the being. It looked like the original form, but not glowing or as big.

Samuel ran down the stairs of the castle and on the way he grabbed his sheathed sword and two knives. He continued running downward until he came out into the yard.

His men had failed to defeat the Second Ishmiel, but he would not.

John watched as the men stopped advancing and stared in fear. John didn't know what they were staring at. He looked behind him, but there was nothing there. John looked back at the men again.

They all fell to the ground for at that moment there was a blinding flash. John covered his face and lay still.

When the light faded John looked up. There was a man with a sword standing there.

John asked him, "Who are you?"

He replied, "I was sent by the Lord to help you. Someone called for a Guardian Angel."

"Angel," John murmured.

"John," the angel said, "I must go now. Always believe."

"Angel," John whispered again.

Only then did John realize that the fight wasn't over yet. He looked toward the castle and saw a man in a black suit with red symbols on his shoulder. He was probably higher ranking like Andrew and the men who bore swords. This man was running, quickly waving his sword over his head.

Dave had finally managed to stand up. He thought back to the man who had appeared. Could it have been an angel?

Dave started limping toward John. Then he saw a man rapidly approaching John, with a sword over his head.

Dave tried to fly to the rescue, but he wasn't strong enough. He picked up a rock and continued his slow, painful limp toward John.

The man had gotten to John by now and they were clashing swords. It didn't look like the man was even trying. John was doing his best to fend off his opponent's blows, but he was inexperienced and the sword was much too heavy for him.

The man was definitely winning.

Dave limped closer as John's strokes slowed, and the man continued to entertain John's efforts. Dave finally got to them and he raised the rock over the man's head.

The man spun around and grabbed Dave's arm. He threw Dave to the ground. John used this moment to smash away the man's weapon. He shouldered into him, and the man came crashing to the ground.

John stood over him, his sword ready to strike. Then the man said. "Kill me if you wish. If you defeat this castle you still haven't defeated us. You can never win. Try to if you wish."

The man said nothing more because John brought the flat side of the blade down on his head.

CHAPTER 8

VOTE

When everyone was awake and healed enough to move around, they started discussing what had happened.

John retold most of it because he was the one who *lasted* the longest. Each one of them told the others about their feelings through the battle.

Then Catherine said, "Well, we won."

That is when they changed the subject. Dave then said "What will we do now?"

"This is off topic, but that's a lot of Ws," John pointed out, "for both of you."

"I hadn't realized that," Dave said thoughtfully.

"I love my alliteration and all, but we have to decide what to do next," Catherine said.

"Yes," agreed Bryan, "we can explore the castle, but there may still be guards, so it would be dangerous. We can go back home and return to our normal lives. Or, we could team up and try to defeat more of the Dark-Ones, though this would be the hardest option of all. All of our powers together make a great team, and me with my gun would help too."

"But what about the kids?" Catherine asked.

"Well," Bryan continued, "Olivia would jump at the opportunity, right Olivia?"

"Right," Olivia responded.

"And I will be Bethanie's personal protector, is that OK Bethanie?" he asked.

"OK," she said.

"Well, I'm sure your son will be OK with it," Bryan said to Dave. "Right John?"

"I guess so," John mumbled. Then much more enthusiastically, "It could be fun!"

"Well, like I said, we probably won't do it anyway," Bryan explained.

"May I make a suggestion?" asked Dave. "We could vote or make a pros and cons list."

"Good idea," Hannah replied.

"First we'll vote, but a pro's and con's list would probably be an unnecessary use of time," Dave said.

Everybody agreed.

"Who votes for exploring the castle?"

John's and Hannah's hands lifted up.

"Two for exploring the castle," Dave said. "Who votes for teaming up to fight?"

Olivia's hand shot up into the air while Bryan's slowly lifted.

"Two for fighting together. And who votes to go home?"

Catherine, Bethanie and Dave put their hands in the air.

"It looks like we're going home," Dave said.

"It's not fair!" John complained. "My hand should count for at least two votes!" John raised his right hand into the air again. He lit a new fireball in his hand and held it high.

"Sorry John," Dave said. "Even someone as special as you only counts as one vote."

"Just because we are going home does not mean that we can't fight together if we have to, and we can keep in touch because we don't live too far away," Catherine explained.

"Yes," said John, "and the man in black said that we could never win, which probably means there are a lot more Dark-Ones, so we definitely will have more adventures."

"Definitely!" Dave agreed. "The adventures will continue."

"I think this will probably be the smallest, but most important adventure of all. How did we even win it?" Catherine said to herself. "All I know is that God definitely helped us in this battle."

"Yes" said John, "you don't know how right you are."

(SEQUEL)

CHAPTER 1

MISTAKE

"Fight! Fight! Fight!"

John wasn't quite sure how he came to be facing off with Sam Slinger, one of the strongest kids in the school.

"So John," he heard Sam taunt, "Are the rumours true? What is it that is different about you? I know there is something wrong with you!"

John knew he could not reveal his power because the Dark-Ones would find him. After the incident almost a year ago he and his family had changed schools and moved halfway across the country, even while his mom was pregnant.

"So, is it true?" Sam continued.

John remained silent. He recognized most of the crowd of students around them. Mike, his best friend, was there. John had even trusted him with his secret of his power.

"Answer me or it could get ugly," threatened Sam.

"I have the right to remain silent," replied John.

"Oh now you go off and name your rights!" Sam said, taking a menacing step forward. "You also have the right to defend yourself."

"Are you sure?" asked Dave. The person on the other end of the phone replied. "Of course, of course," Dave agreed, "I'll tell Catherine and we'll come right away. Goodbye." He put down the phone.

"Who was it?" asked Catherine, taking care of their newborn baby girl, Zoe. Zoe was over three months old now.

"It was Bryan, and he said that the Dark-Ones have a castle in the Antarctic, and they are preparing to destroy us. They have created a powerful weapon, but I don't know what it is," Dave replied.

"Well, if we have to leave," said Catherine, "we will have to get a trustworthy babysitter."

"Will Jenny do?" asked Dave.

"Yes, I trust her," replied Catherine.

"OK, I'll call her."

While Dave called Jenny, Catherine got ready for the trip.

Sam lunged toward John. John rolled out of the way, just in time. He got up barely avoiding another punch. John realized that if he would have any chance in this fight, he would have to fight back. He tried to tackle Sam, but it just resulted with a shove and him toppling backwards.

Sam tried to pin him down, but John kicked hard and hit his stomach. He fell on the ground, but got back up. This gave John time to get up too. Sam was in pain, John could see it, but he was trying to hide it from the onlookers.

Sam lunged again and John dodged, but Sam's nails sunk deep in his left arm. John stumbled back in agony.

John straightened and took a step forward. Some of the audience stared wide-eyed as the scratch healed, almost immediately.

John charged forward and with his momentum, plowed into Sam. They both fell over with John on top of Sam. Then Sam rolled over and pinned John to the ground.

"So, now are you gonna admit it?" Sam jeered.

"Admit what?" John asked.

"You know what!" Sam yelled. "If you admit and tell us, I'll let you go. If you don't, I will do otherwise."

John struggled under Sam's weight, but it was no use.

John couldn't tell them about his power. He would have to resist. He pushed as hard as he possibly could. He was concentrating so hard and getting so angry that he messed up. He let out a flame.

The small flame crawled up Sam's shirt, but as soon as John saw it, he put it out. As well as creating fire, he could also control it.

There was one kid in the crowd that saw it though, and he ran off.

'Jimmy', thought John, 'the biggest rumour starter in the whole school. He saw my flame. This would start new crazy rumours about me.'

But the flame did something. It burnt Sam. Sam got off John and John took the opportunity to stand up.

Some people cheered because John had hurt Sam, the school bully.

While the fight continued, John thought about the flame and about Jimmy. Only one person had seen it and most people wouldn't believe him. But John knew that any small mistake, like this, could mean disaster.

Printed in the United States
By Bookmasters